CHOOSE YOUR

STAR WARS™

A FINN & POE ADVENTURE

WRITTEN BY
CAVAN SCOTT

ILLUSTRATED BY
ELSA CHARRETIER

DISNEP

LUCASFILM
PRESS

LOS ANGELES • NEW YORK

For information address Disney • Lucasfilm Press,
1200 Grand Central Avenue, Glendale, California 91201.
Printed in the United States of America
First Paperback Edition, October 2019
1 3 5 7 9 10 8 6 4 2
FAC-029261-19225
ISBN 978-1-368-04338-0
Library of Congress Control Number on file
Designed by Leigh Zieske

SUSTAINABLE
FORESTRY
INITIATIVE

Certified Sourcing

www.sfiprogram.org
SFI-01415

Visit the official *Star Wars* website at: www.starwars.com.

» ATTENTION, READER

Finn, Poe, and BB-8 are three of the Resistance's greatest heroes—but they need your help!

This book is full of choices—choices that lead to different adventures, choices that you must make to help Finn, Poe, and BB-8.

Do not read the following pages straight through from start to finish! When you are asked to make a choice, follow the instructions to see where that choice will lead Finn, Poe, and BB-8 next.

CHOOSE CAREFULLY.

AND MAY THE FORCE BE WITH YOU!

A LONG TIME AGO
IN A GALAXY FAR, FAR
AWAY. . . ..

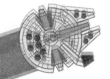

"POE—WHAT'S HAPPENED?"

Finn raced into the *StarRover*'s cockpit as the tiny freighter dropped out of hyperspace without warning. A wedge-shaped cruiser filled the viewport, its many cannons slowly turning to face them.

"That's the First Order!"

"I noticed," Poe replied, wiggling the flight yoke. The *Rover* didn't respond. The Resistance pilot glanced over his shoulder at the orange-and-white astromech that was rolling back and forth trying to reboot consoles that remained stubbornly quiet. "Any luck, Beebee-Ate?"

The droid responded with a frantic series of beeps. The *StarRover* was completely dead.

None of this made sense. One second they had been zooming through hyperspace, and the next they were marooned in front of an enemy ship.

"Is it the hyperdrive?" Finn asked, dropping into the copilot seat.

"No," Poe said, checking a readout above his head. "The First Order has mined the hyper route with

gravity-well generators powerful enough to snare a Dreadnought."

Finn glanced through the viewport. Poe was right. The space in front of them was scattered with debris from a dozen ships.

"Can't we turn around?" Finn asked.

"We can't do anything," Poe admitted, jumping up to check a nearby terminal. "The sudden stop shorted out the *StarRover's* systems. Navigation. Shields. Propulsion. They're all gone."

"But we still have life support?"

"We're breathing, aren't we? But we won't be for long. The environmental regulator is hanging on by a thread, and the gravity generator . . . well, let's just say it's a miracle we're not floating."

Finn swallowed hard as he spotted a flashing light on the comlink. That would be the cruiser's commander, ordering their surrender.

"Please tell me the weapons are still operational."

Poe flashed him a grin as he slipped back behind the flight controls. "This ship came from Maz Kanata. What do you expect?"

So it wasn't all bad. The notorious pirate queen had supplied the *StarRover* so Finn and Poe could travel to Tevel, home to one of the New Republic's last remaining bacta plants. According to C-3PO, the First Order had annexed the planet, and the Tevellans had appealed to what was left of the Resistance for help. In return, they had promised General Organa a supply of much-needed bacta. The gelatinous substance could cure just about any injury, from cuts and grazes to broken bones, a necessity when waging war against an enemy as brutal as the First Order.

The light on the dashboard continued to blink.

"Should we answer that?"

Poe shook his head. "I think we have bigger problems."

Finn followed his gaze to see a huge First Order space station in the distance. A trio of TIE fighters were shrieking toward them, cannons already running hot.

WHAT SHOULD THEY DO?

ATTACK THE TIE FIGHTERS—TURN TO PAGE 16.
BUY THEMSELVES TIME BY FAKING A COMPLETE SYSTEM FAILURE—GO TO PAGE 8.

"THIS WAY," Poe said, leading Finn and BB-8 toward what appeared to be a perfectly normal panel in the wall until it slid open to reveal a secret compartment. It was hardly larger than a maintenance closet, but it was just about big enough for all three of them to squeeze into it.

Now what? Finn mouthed as they heard stormtroopers enter the cockpit.

ATTACK THE STORMTROOPERS—GO TO PAGE 20.

SNEAK OUT WHEN THE STORMTROOPERS AREN'T LOOKING—TURN TO PAGE 7.

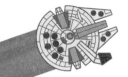

"CAN'T WE DO SOMETHING?" Finn asked.

"Sure we can," Poe said, slapping him on the shoulder. "We can escape."

He swiveled around to face BB-8.

"We need those engines working, pal."

BB-8 bleeped a reply and went to work. Poe shouted out excitedly when propulsion came back online.

"Hold on," he said, gripping the flight controls. "This is going to be rough."

"How rough?" Finn asked.

Poe's only answer was to gun the engines in an attempt to escape the tractor beam's hold. The power core whined, and sparks flew from every console. Poe gritted his teeth as if he was trying to pull them free himself.

BB-8 squealed as power lines ruptured, fires breaking out across the ship.

GO TO PAGE 54.

POE INDICATED for them to wait until the troopers had finished examining the cockpit. Then, when they were sure the coast was clear, they slipped out of their hidey-hole and crept through the ship.

The stormtroopers had cleared out, but the ship was still docked in a First Order space station. Where exactly were they supposed to go?

Poe smiled. "Don't worry, pal. There's more than one way off this ship."

He led them to the rear of the freighter and pressed a control on a bulkhead, causing another secret panel to slide open.

"How many panic rooms did Maz install on this thing?" Finn asked, peering down the ladder Poe had revealed.

"More than you'll ever know," Poe said, already clambering down to a hatch in the belly of the ship.

WHAT SHOULD THEY DO?

TRY TO SEND A MESSAGE TO THE RESISTANCE—GO TO PAGE 11.

STEAL A SHIP AND ESCAPE—TURN TO PAGE 52.

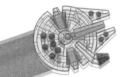

"BEEBEE-ATE," Poe said, "fire up the concussion missiles."

"No," Finn cut in before the astromech could respond. "You said we had no thrusters or shields. We won't stand a chance against TIE fighters. Shut everything down."

Poe's eyebrows shot up. "What?"

"Think about it," Finn reasoned. "Why fire on a ship with total system failure?"

A grin spread across Poe's face.

"You heard the man, buddy. Shut everything down. Environmental systems. Lights. Everything."

The droid let out a worried bloop but did as he was told as Poe threw a portable breathing mask toward Finn.

Finn caught the mask, strapped it over his nose and mouth, and then had to grab the arms of his chair to stop himself from floating up as the antigrav generator powered down.

The cockpit was plunged into darkness, the *StarRover* eerily quiet.

The TIE fighters streaked closer by the second, and Finn hoped he'd been right.

They wouldn't fire on a critically damaged ship . . . would they?

"Use the time to repair the systems," Poe whispered to BB-8, as if the fighter pilots could somehow hear him over the empty void of space.

Finn's grip on his chair tightened as they closed in. The fighters were still in attack formation.

Why weren't they peeling off?

"Maybe this wasn't such a great idea," Poe said, resting his hands on the weapon controls. "Beebee-Ate, it looks like we're gonna need those missiles after all."

"No, wait," Finn said, placing a hand on Poe's arm. The TIE fighters changed course, breaking formation to fly straight past the *StarRover*.

"They bought it!" Poe exclaimed, punching Finn in the arm. "We're still in the game!"

The *Rover* started moving steadily toward the space station.

Finn frowned.

"Is that you, Beebee-Ate? Are the thrusters back online?"

He didn't need a computer to translate the droid's mournful reply.

"It's a tractor beam," Poe reported. "They're reeling us in."

WHAT SHOULD THEY DO?

TRY TO BREAK FREE OF THE TRACTOR BEAM—TURN TO PAGE 6.

FIGHT BACK—GO TO PAGE 26.

LET THEMSELVES BE HAULED IN—TURN TO PAGE 18.

"WE NEED TO WARN LEIA that this place exists," Poe said, glancing around the hangar. "Those gravity mines could bring down half the fleet."

"Then we need a comm station," Finn said, leading them to a computer terminal hidden behind a TIE cradle. BB-8 inserted a connector and piggybacked the message on official First Order transmissions, squealing excitedly before disconnecting.

"Keep it down, pal," Poe said, his eyes going wide as the droid showed him what he'd found. The First Order was keeping a group of prisoners in the station, former senators who had escaped Starkiller Base's destruction of Hosnian Prime.

"Just imagine if we rescued them," Poe said. "They could raise support for the Resistance on countless worlds. What do you think?"

SHOULD THEY RESCUE THE SENATORS?

YES—TURN TO PAGE 30.
NO—TURN TO PAGE 27.

POE'S HAND WENT FOR his blaster, but Finn stopped him.

"Easy there, pal," Finn whispered. "I have an idea. Wait here."

Finn disappeared into a nearby maintenance closet.

"You've got to be kidding me," Poe said when he reemerged carrying two sonic mops.

"Don't knock it," Finn said. "Janitors can go almost anywhere."

Poe reluctantly took one of the mops. Finn always trusted Poe when he had a crazy idea. It was time for Poe to do the same.

Proving Finn's point, the officer barely looked up as the whine of the mops filled the detention block, only taking notice when Poe's mop head bumped the computer desk.

"Hey, watch it, will you?" the lieutenant barked, looking up from his work.

When the officer saw Poe's jacket, he jumped to his feet.

"Hey! That's not regulation uniform!"

"No," Finn said, swinging his sonic mop with purpose, "it's not."

The officer grunted as Finn took his legs out from under him, knocking him out on the highly polished floor.

"He won't be down for long," Finn warned.

HOW DO THEY GET THE PRISONERS OUT OF THEIR CELLS?

TRY TO ENTER A CODE—GO TO PAGE 29.

HAVE BB-8 OVERRIDE THE LOCKS—HEAD TO PAGE 55.

"WHAT DO WE DO?" Finn said, spinning around at the sound of the approaching boots.

"Isn't it obvious?" Poe said, gripping his blaster in both hands and waiting for the first trooper to come barreling around the corner. "We fight."

Maybe that wasn't the best course of action, Finn thought as he woke later, his head muggy with the effects of a stun beam. He looked around, taking in his surroundings. The cell was barren and completely escape-proof. Now *he* was the one in need of a rescue.

THE END

CAN YOU GO BACK AND MAKE BETTER DECISIONS?

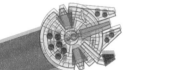

"GET ME AS MANY WEAPONS as you can,
buddy!" Poe shouted to BB-8, rerouting defensive
controls to the cockpit's forward station.

"Finn, you take the primary laser cannon, and I'll
handle the missiles."

Finn grabbed the controls, his eyes darting across
the lights that had blinked on in front of him.

"Are you sure this is going to be enough, Poe? You
said we had no thrusters."

"We don't."

"Then how are we supposed to outmaneuver
starfighters?"

It was a good question and one Poe couldn't answer
as laser fire streamed from the nearest TIE.

Poe locked on to the fighter's signal and sent
missiles screaming across the void.

They found their target, the TIE dissolving in
a storm of light and supercharged metal, but the
remaining fighters continued on an attack vector.

Finn swung in his chair, thumbing the laser controls,
but he couldn't find either of the darting ships.

The two TIE pilots fired as one, lasers slamming into Maz's ship.

The deck lurched as a series of explosions shook the small craft.

TURN TO PAGE 54.

"WHAT'RE WE GONNA DO?" Finn asked as
the space station grew larger by the second in their
viewport.

"Hold our nerve," Poe said.

"And let ourselves be captured?"

"They don't know we're even in here."

"They would have scanned for life signs," Finn told
him.

"And they wouldn't have found any. Maz installed
scramblers before we left. The First Order won't know
we're here unless they board us."

"And what happens if they do?"

Poe checked the charge on his blaster. "We
improvise."

Finn tried to breathe normally as the *Rover* was
hauled into the station's vast hangar bay. Poe was
so composed, so sure of himself, even as he saw a
squadron of stormtroopers waiting for them, blasters
in hand.

Not long before, Finn would have been among
them, standing in gleaming armor, waiting for the
enemies of the First Order to be brought to justice. But

he was done with that life. Finn tried to be brave, but the truth was that he was still scared.

Scared that he wouldn't be good enough.

Scared that he would let everyone down.

Poe and Leia had been born into this fight, their lives defined by the struggles against the First Order and the Empire before it. Finn, on the other, had stumbled into the Resistance. He believed in what they stood for, of course, but even after everything they'd been through, he still struggled to believe in himself.

But this wasn't the time for doubts. Finn settled back into his chair as the space station's artificial gravity took hold of them. With a thud, the *StarRover* touched down, the tractor beam depositing them with typical First Order efficiency.

The stormtroopers were already marching toward the freighter. The *Rover* would be boarded in minutes.

WHAT SHOULD FINN AND POE DO?

HIDE THEMSELVES ON THE SHIP—TURN TO PAGE 5.

TRY TO ESCAPE WITHOUT BEING SEEN—GO TO PAGE 22.

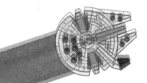

"THIS!" POE SHOUTED, drawing his blaster and reopening the secret door to fire on the unsuspecting First Order stormtroopers.

Finn was in awe of Poe's bravery. The pilot was skilled with a blaster and quickly managed to take down the nearest trooper, but he soon lost the element of surprise and was firing out of what amounted to a cupboard. And there was nothing that Finn or BB-8 could do to help.

With nowhere to retreat, Poe was outgunned as the remaining stormtroopers filled the secret compartment with stun fire.

Finn awoke to find himself in a harness. He tried to pull free, but the restraints were locked tight.

He looked around, realizing that he was on a First Order shuttle, the pilots sitting with their back to him at the controls. He went instinctively for his blaster, but it was gone.

"There's no point trying to escape, traitor," one of the pilots said, swiveling in her chair to face him.

"We're taking you to the Supreme Leader for

questioning," the other pilot added. "He's looking forward to talking to you."

I bet he is, Finn thought, hoping that Poe and BB-8 had gotten away.

It was unlikely, but hope was all he had left.

THE END

CAN YOU GO BACK AND MAKE BETTER DECISIONS?

FINN YANKED his breathing mask from his face and drew his blaster. The whine of a fusioncutter echoed through the cruiser as the stormtroopers sliced through the *Rover*'s hatch. Beside him, BB-8 flicked out an arc welder, the closest thing to a weapon the tiny droid possessed.

Poe smiled at his friends. "Stand down, boys. We're not going to fight them."

"We're not?" Finn said as Poe hurried them from the cockpit.

"No. We're going to be sneaky."

He pressed a control on the wall, and a panel in the ship's corridor slid open.

Finn grinned as he peered down the ladder it had revealed. "I like sneaky. Where does this lead?"

"To the ventral hatch."

"There's another way out?"

"In the belly of the ship." Poe placed a boot on the ladder. "You coming?"

Before Finn could follow, BB-8 barged past, extending telescopic arms to clatter down behind the pilot.

"After you . . ." Finn grumbled before climbing down himself.

"What are we going to do when we get outside?" he whispered as the hidden panel slid back into place, sealing them in the secret shaft.

Poe raised an eyebrow. "What do you think?"

Finn laughed. "Right, we improvise. What else is new?"

WHAT SHOULD THEY DO?

SEND A MESSAGE TO THE RESISTANCE—GO TO PAGE 11.

STEAL A SHIP TO ESCAPE—TURN TO PAGE 52.

"WE'RE GONNA NEED all the help we can get,"
Poe said, instructing BB-8 to free everyone. It was a
good call. Most of the senators were struggling to walk,
although the pirates and smugglers were more able.

Poe marshaled them, convincing scoundrels and
rogues to help the very senators who had once passed
laws against them. Everyone was united against a
common enemy, although Finn did have to stop the
bounty hunter from blasting the unconscious security
guard out of pure spite.

"We don't want to attract attention to ourselves,
okay?"

But there was no escaping the alarms that soon
wailed through the base. The freed prisoners ran,
the able helping the weak, while Poe and Finn took
care of any stormtroopers who stood in their way.
The smugglers and pirates happily scooped up the
discarded weapons.

Not everyone made it back to the hangar. The
bounty hunter had even sacrificed herself so Finn and
Poe could bundle the survivors on board a nearby med
shuttle.

Dropping into the pilot seat, Poe gunned the engine, and the shuttle streamed from the station before the First Order could lock on with its tractor beam. TIE fighters were already in pursuit when Poe made the jump to hyperspace, heading not for Tevel but back to the Resistance. They may not have secured any bacta, but the rescue of the senators would please Leia. Any victory against the First Order was a cause for celebration.

**YOU'VE DONE WELL, BUT AN EVEN
GREATER DESTINY AWAITS YOU.**

WHY NOT GO BACK AND TRY A DIFFERENT PATH?

"WE CAN TAKE OUT the tractor beam," Poe said, activating the targeting computer.

"What?" Finn spluttered. "How?"

"By destroying the emitter. Beebee-Ate, scan the station for the focusing array."

"Surely this can't work," Finn said as BB-8 provided the target.

"Sure, it will," Poe said, mashing the triggers.

The *Rover* unloaded its laser cannons into the station, but the tractor beam still held.

"Then again . . ."

Finn threw up a hand to protect his eyes as the First Order returned fire, the sudden glare of turbolaser blasts blinding them as the ship shook under the barrage.

GO TO PAGE 54.

FINN SHOOK HIS HEAD. "It's too risky. Getting off this station will be hard enough. It would be better to complete our mission and then come back with the support of the fleet. The prisoners aren't exactly going anywhere."

Poe sighed. "You're right. One thing at a time. We steal a ship, head to Tevel, and tell Leia about the senators once we get back to the Resistance."

Finn laughed. "You make it sound so easy. Remember the last time we stole a ship?"

"We got away, didn't we?" Poe said before bolting across the deck.

"Got away?" Finn and BB-8 followed the pilot, ducking behind a weapons rack. "We nearly died!"

WHICH SHIP SHOULD THEY STEAL?

A TIE FIGHTER—GO TO PAGE 34.
A MED SHUTTLE—TURN TO PAGE 32.

"WE NEED TO GET OUT of here," Poe said, dragging Finn after him before the troopers could arrive.

"But what about the prisoners?"

"We'll come back for them," Poe promised, "and we'll bring reinforcements. In the meantime, we need to get off this station. Maybe we can still complete our mission and get to Tevel."

"How?" Finn asked as they ran to the hangar bay.

"Easy. We steal a ship."

Finn laughed, remembering how the two of them had first met, trying to escape the First Order's *Finalizer* in a stolen TIE fighter.

"Because that went *so* well the last time."

"We got away, didn't we?" Poe said before bolting across the bay.

"Got away?" Finn and BB-8 followed the pilot, ducking behind a weapons rack. "We nearly died!"

WHICH SHIP SHOULD THEY STEAL?

A TIE FIGHTER—GO TO PAGE 34.

A MED SHUTTLE—TURN TO PAGE 32.

THE LIEUTENANT moaned as Poe tried to open the cells.

"They're protected by a code."

Finn glanced down at the stunned man. "He's not about to tell us what it is."

Poe started typing random numbers, the computer beeping with every keystroke.

"You can't guess," Finn told him. "There must be a thousand different combinations."

"But only one alarm," Poe groaned as a warning rang out on his third attempt.

"Drop your weapons," the stormtroopers barked as they ran into the detention cells.

Finn threw his mop to the floor, followed by his blaster.

Soon they'd be in cells of their own.

THE END

CAN YOU GO BACK AND MAKE BETTER DECISIONS?

"LET'S DO IT," Finn said, trying to appear more confident than he felt as BB-8 searched for the prisoners' location.

Soon they were peering around a corner deep in the heart of the space station, looking through a set of glass doors at the detention block's security guard.

HOW DO THEY GET PAST THE GUARD?

BLAST THEIR WAY IN—HEAD TO PAGE 53.

TRICK THEIR WAY IN—TURN TO PAGE 12.

"WE ONLY NEED THE SENATORS," Finn said. "Better to cause as small a scene as possible."

Seconds later, Finn, Poe, and BB-8 were trying to usher the former officials out of the cells. The only problem was that most of the senators were barely strong enough to walk, let alone run to the hangar bay.

"We need to move quicker," Finn said, forced to carry a particularly fragile Tarsunt.

"You're telling me," Poe agreed as they stumbled out of the detention block.

No one noticed the security officer groggily hitting a panic switch, but there was no missing the alarm that blared through the corridors.

Hampered by the senator, Finn tried to grab his blaster but couldn't draw it in time to stop the stormtroopers that streamed into the block.

Perhaps they should have freed everyone, after all.

THE END

CAN YOU GO BACK AND MAKE BETTER DECISIONS?

"SO THIS TIME we'll take something better than a TIE fighter," Poe whispered, peeking around the weapons rack.

"Like what?"

"Like *that*." Poe nodded toward a blocky ship docked on the other side of the hangar. Personnel wearing long white coats were loading crates into the stout craft's cargo bay.

"A med shuttle?"

Poe shrugged. "We *are* going to a bacta plant. It's the perfect cover."

That made sense, but how were they going to get on board?

HOW DO THEY GET ON BOARD THE SHUTTLE?

BLAST THEIR WAY IN—GO TO PAGE 43.

PRETEND TO BE MEDICAL STAFF—TURN TO PAGE 35.

POE WAS ALREADY RUNNING for a TIE interceptor. Finn helped BB-8 into the cockpit while alarms blared across the hangar bay. Poe fired up the ion engines, and the starfighter screamed off into the safety of hyperspace.

"We did it!" Finn whooped. "We actually did it!"

"We absolutely did," Poe agreed, "although there's one small problem. We don't have enough fuel to get to Tevel."

Finn couldn't believe it. After all that, they'd have to head back to the Resistance empty-handed?

"Hey, keep your spirits up," Poe said. "At least we can learn the capabilities of this fighter. That's a good thing, right?"

Poe was right. Any victory against the First Order was a cause for celebration, but that didn't mean Finn was looking forward to telling Leia what had happened. . . .

THE END

CAN YOU GO BACK AND MAKE BETTER DECISIONS?

"WHERE CAN WE GET some of those coats?" Poe asked.

"There," Finn said, pointing at a storage room near the shuttle. "But we're bound to be spotted."

With a defiant bleep, BB-8 broke cover, trundling across the hangar as if he was in command.

"That's my droid!" Poe laughed as they ran after him. "Man, has he got guts."

"Or a death wish!"

They darted from one hiding place to another, crouching behind a fleet transport before sprinting for the thick legs of a scout walker. Soon they were only meters from the storage room, a sloping TIE fighter ramp providing cover. They waited for the last of the med crew to leave before scooting inside.

"My mom always wanted me to be a doctor," Poe said wistfully, slipping on the pristine white coat he'd just taken from a peg.

"I think you should stick to flying," Finn replied, grabbing a coat of his own. "But what're we going to do with Beebee-Ate?"

Poe nodded toward an open equipment crate. "Simple. We put him in one of those!"

The astromech wasted no time telling Poe what he thought of that plan.

"Come on, buddy," Poe said, dropping onto a knee beside the droid. "It's not like you're claustrophobic. It won't be long, I promise."

Still grumbling, BB-8 allowed them to lift him into the crate.

"Now keep quiet," Poe said, closing the lid. Activating the crate's repulsorlifts, Poe and Finn pushed BB-8 out of the storage room, trying their hardest not to look suspicious. As they approached the shuttle, Finn glanced back at the *StarRover*. The troopers were reporting to their captain. Had they found the secret exit? He increased his pace, nearly slamming BB-8's crate into the back of a muscle-bound medic who looked more likely to break bones than fix them.

"Hey, watch it, will ya."

"Yeah, look where you're going!" Poe snapped at Finn before their cover could be blown. He shook his head, playing the despairing superior. "Sorry, big guy. I don't know what they teach at the academy these days."

Still scowling, the disgruntled medic limped back to the storeroom.

"Thanks," Finn whispered as they pushed the crate up the shuttle's ramp. "I owe you."

"Don't mention it," Poe replied as they were met by an MD-series medical droid with a datapad in its pincers.

"What is that?" the robot said, peering at their container before checking its list. "According to the manifest, everything has already been loaded. You'll have to take it back."

WHAT DO THEY SAY?

"I DON'T KNOW WHAT IT IS. HANG ON, I'LL JUST TAKE A LOOK." TURN TO PAGE 40.
"WHAT ARE YOU TALKING ABOUT? YOUR LIST MUST BE WRONG." GO TO PAGE 60.

"HEAD FOR THE PLANT," Poe said, breaking into a run to put as much distance as possible between them and whatever lurked in the grass.

"Won't they wonder why we're here?" Finn asked, matching Poe step for step.

Poe slipped his blaster beneath his white coat. "We're medical personnel, remember? Just follow my lead."

Sure enough, the major in charge of the base looked surprised to see two medics and an orange-and-white astromech racing out of the grass.

"Who are you?" he asked, a silver seeker droid bobbing in the air behind him.

Poe gasped, trying to catch his breath. "Our shuttle came down in the field. Didn't you see?"

The stern-faced officer shook his head. "No, I'm afraid I didn't. Tell me, why are you here?"

WHAT DO THEY SAY?

"WE'RE HERE TO INSPECT THE PLANT." TURN TO PAGE 59.

"WE'RE HERE TO PICK UP BACTA FOR A
MEDICAL EMERGENCY." GO TO PAGE 46.

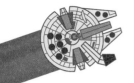

MINUTES LATER, Finn and Poe were staring at the flickering hologram of a very familiar face.

"Fool," Kylo Ren bellowed at the major. "These are Resistance agents. Arrest them at once."

Varak fumbled for his blaster, all too aware that he was being watched by the Supreme Leader.

DO THEY FIGHT BACK?

YES—GO TO PAGE 69.
NO—TURN TO PAGE 66.

POE SHRUGGED. "I don't know what it is." He went to open the lid. "Hang on, I'll just take a look."

"No, no, no," the medical droid said, shooing him away. "Let me. You organics can't be trusted."

"Charming," Poe said, winking at Finn as the droid flicked open the lid to reveal BB-8.

"What are *you* doing in there?" the med droid asked before BB-8 replied by thrusting an electro-shock prod into the MD's extended pincers. The droid's datapad clattered to the deck as its circuits fried. Finn caught the droid before it could topple over, then bundled it into the crate, which BB-8 had happily vacated. The astromech made straight for an access point and closed the cargo bay's door.

"Do you think there's anyone else on board?" Finn asked.

"Let's find out," Poe said, opening another crate to find a supply of hydrospray.

Keeping quiet, they crept to the cockpit and spotted the pilot preparing for takeoff.

"We ready to roll, Emdee?" the pilot asked, mistaking Poe's footsteps for the medical droid's.

"Yeah, but you're not coming," Poe said, spraying

the pilot's face with the sedative. The pilot slumped forward and was snoring peacefully by the time they laid him in another crate next to the med droid.

"What're we going to do with them?" Finn asked as he closed the lid, leaving enough of a gap that air could get through to the snoozing pilot.

"Leave them behind," Poe replied, opening the hatch so they could push the container outside.

With their unwanted cargo unloaded, Finn and Poe rushed back to the cockpit, where BB-8 was already priming the engines. Poe took his place behind the flight controls and requested permission to depart.

Soon they were slipping through the hangar doors and out into open space.

"That wasn't too difficult, was it?" Poe asked as a voice crackled over the shuttle's comm.

"*Med Shuttle Two-Seven-Oh-Five, please respond.*"

Poe ignored the command, activating the hyperdrive instead. "Beebee-Ate, set course for Tevel."

The droid plugged a connector into the navicomputer as the station master attempted to contact them again.

"*You have left cargo in the hangar, Two-Seven-Oh-Five. Please respond immediately.*"

"How long before they look inside?" Finn asked. "You know they'll blame the pilot."

Poe grinned, reaching for the hyperjump lever. "Serves him right for sleeping on the job."

He pulled back hard, sending the shuttle shooting into hyperspace.

GO TO PAGE 44.

"LET'S GO!" Poe said, drawing his blaster. They ran up the ramp, and Poe stunned a startled medical officer before heading for the cockpit. "You seal the hatch, and I'll get us out of here."

Finn rushed to the controls but was cut off by stormtrooper blasts from outside. He ducked behind the crates and returned fire, not noticing the medical droid shuffling up behind him.

His first—and last—clue was the hiss of the sedative as an injector was pressed up against his neck. His eyes rolled back in their sockets, and he slumped to the floor.

THE END

CAN YOU GO BACK AND MAKE BETTER DECISIONS?

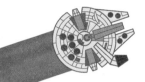

IT WASN'T LONG before they were dropping into the atmosphere of Tevel, a small planet on the very edge of First Order space.

According to the briefing C-3PO had given them before they left the Resistance base, Tevel was sparsely populated, with most Tevellans living on the nearby moon.

The planet itself was largely agricultural, the land given over to the crops required to produce bacta. The primary production facility was located in the northern hemisphere.

It wasn't hard to spot against the gently swaying grasslands: rows of gigantic cylindrical tanks, each containing liters of bacta ready to be shipped across the galaxy, arranged around a central courtyard.

There were a number of prefabricated buildings among the tanks, which Finn assumed held refineries, as well as facilities for the staff—although even from that distance the plant looked deserted, no one bustling from building to building or going about their work.

Finn assumed that had something to do with the

towering AT-AT walker that stood at the center of the complex, or the row of TIE fighters docked at the very edge of the plant.

**WHERE SHOULD THEY TRY TO LAND
WHEN THEY ARRIVE ON TEVEL?**

**AT THE BACTA PLANT—TURN TO PAGE 48.
IN THE SURROUNDING GRASSLANDS—GO TO PAGE 51.**

"WE'RE HERE TO PICK UP BACTA for a medical emergency in the Mid Rim," Poe said, thinking on his feet.

They'll never buy that, Finn thought, and then he had to try to hide his surprise when the officer said, "Of course."

Before long, stormtroopers were loading barrels of fresh bacta onto the shuttle. Poe offered to help, but the plant's commander wouldn't hear of it.

"You have a long journey ahead of you. Where is the emergency?"

Finn jumped in, saying the first name he could think of. "Um . . . Nordis Prime."

"A terrible tragedy," the major said, as if he knew what Finn was talking about. He must have gotten lucky and named the location of a *real* disaster.

Finn still couldn't believe it as Poe piloted the shuttle back to the Resistance. "That was too easy."

"No one ever said the First Order was intelligent."

"But that's just it, Poe. They are—ruthlessly intelligent. I don't like this."

Poe signaled the Resistance base as they drew

nearer so they wouldn't be shot down. "Look, we've been through a lot recently. It's about time something went our way."

But the pilot's good humor floundered as they opened the barrels after landing.

"They're empty," Finn said, but Poe shook his head.

"No, they're not. There are weights inside, so they felt like they were full of bacta."

"And that's not all," said General Organa, marching up to them. "We've picked up a homing signal coming from the base."

"Whose base?" Finn asked. "Our base?"

Leia reached inside the nearest barrel to pull out a tiny beacon. "This is enough to bring the entire First Order to our door. We need to abandon the base and start again." She threw the beacon back into the container in frustration. "They knew who you were, Poe. This will set us back months."

THE END

CAN YOU GO BACK AND MAKE BETTER DECISIONS?

THE COMM BUZZED as Finn and Poe approached, a First Order petty officer asking for their authorization codes.

"What if they've found the pilot? Should we try to just land in those grasslands and sneak into the plant?" Finn asked as BB-8 transmitted the codes he'd discovered in the shuttle's main computer.

"We're a long way from the station," Poe replied, maintaining their flight path. "I doubt they've alerted bases all the way out here."

Sure enough, the ident codes were accepted and Poe was instructed to bring the shuttle down on a nearby landing pad.

"Follow my lead," Poe said once they'd touched down. He pulled his medical coat tight as he marched down the landing ramp. They were greeted by a sour-faced officer wearing a teal uniform. The major was flanked not only by a pair of stormtroopers but by a multilimbed seeker droid that hovered near him like an obedient pet.

"Lieutenant," the officer said, spying the insignia on Poe's sleeve. "This is an unexpected pleasure."

Poe frowned, feigning surprise. "You weren't told to expect us?"

The officer shook his head, peering at them down his long, haughty nose. "No, I'm afraid not. Tell me, why are you here?"

WHAT DO THEY SAY?

"WE ARE HERE TO INSPECT THE PLANT." TURN TO PAGE 59.

"WE'RE HERE TO PICK UP BACTA FOR A MEDICAL EMERGENCY." GO TO PAGE 46.

"SHOULD WE land at the plant itself?" Finn asked, but Poe shook his head, eyeing the heavily armored First Order walker standing guard.

"Let's not announce our presence just yet."

He brought the shuttle down in the high grass that Finn assumed was used in the production of the bacta. They disembarked, still wearing the long coats, and the crop was as tall as they were.

Suddenly, they heard a growl behind them.

"What's that?" Finn asked, spinning around.

Poe drew his blaster. "Not sure. Keep your eyes open."

"Thanks. I hadn't thought of that."

Something rustled through the grass—something big, moving fast.

Finn instantly regretted leaving the shuttle.

"Should we go back?"

WHERE SHOULD THEY GO?

BACK TO THE SHIP—GO TO PAGE 56.

HEAD TO THE PLANT—TURN TO PAGE 38.

"OKAY," FINN SAID, peering over Poe's shoulder as the pilot closed the hatch in the belly of the ship behind them. "Any ideas?"

"Sure. We steal a ship."

Finn rolled his eyes. "Oh, because that went *so* well last time."

The pair had met running from the First Order in a stolen TIE fighter. They'd escaped a Star Destroyer only to be shot down over Jakku.

"We got away, didn't we?" Poe said before bolting across the deck.

"Got away?" Finn and BB-8 followed the pilot, ducking behind a weapons rack. "We nearly died!"

WHICH SHIP SHOULD THEY STEAL?

A TIE FIGHTER—GO TO PAGE 34.

A MED SHUTTLE—TURN TO PAGE 32.

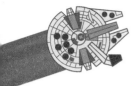

POE PULLED HIS BLASTER, stunning the officer with a single shot, but the lieutenant's stunted cry was enough to bring stormtroopers running.

DO FINN AND POE FIGHT BACK OR TRY TO ESCAPE?

FIGHT BACK—GO TO PAGE 15.

TRY TO ESCAPE—TURN TO PAGE 28.

"WE NEED TO ABANDON SHIP!" Finn yelled, all but dragging Poe from the pilot's chair.

For a moment, he worried that his friend was going to stay where he was, trying to find a way, however improbable, to turn the tables on the First Order. Thankfully, even Poe Dameron knew when to bail out of a fight.

They ran to the escape pod, BB-8 rolling at their heels. After they'd all squeezed into the cramped capsule, Poe released the clamps. The pod spun out into space before the ship erupted in flames.

"What if they scan for life signs?" Finn asked.

Poe reminded him about Maz's scramblers. "They'll think it's a faulty pod . . . probably."

Finn rested his head on his knees. He knew the drill. They would float until they'd reached a safe distance and then transmit a distress signal. The mission had failed before it had even truly begun.

THE END

CAN YOU GO BACK AND MAKE BETTER DECISIONS?

54

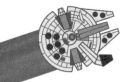

"OVER TO YOU, BUDDY," Poe said, standing aside so BB-8 could access the computer.

Finn checked a screen as BB-8 connected himself. "There are more than just senators here. The First Order has everyone from pirates to smugglers locked in those cells. . . . There's even a bounty hunter!"

WHICH PRISONERS SHOULD THEY RELEASE?

JUST THE SENATORS—TURN TO PAGE 31.
ALL OF THEM—GO TO PAGE 24.

THERE WAS THE GROWL AGAIN, nearer than before.

BB-8 was already rolling back the way they'd come.

"I think he's got the right idea," Finn said, racing after the droid only to see the astromech be attacked by a large cat with tusks. BB-8 squealed as the beast bit down on his head, pulling it from his helplessly spinning body.

"Hey, that's my droid!" Poe yelled, drawing his blaster. The cat whirled around, both of its tails whipping through the air as it pounced toward him.

After making sure his blaster was on stun, Poe emptied his power pack into the beast, but the shots seemed to have no effect. The striped monster finally collapsed with the last shot, snoring as if it was taking a catnap in the sun. Poe was in a bad state, though, the animal's claws having raked through his clothes.

BB-8 had survived the attack and clamped his head back onto his dented body.

"Get us out of here!" Finn yelled as he laid Poe on the floor of the shuttle and went to rifle through the medical supplies.

He attended Poe's wounds as BB-8 piloted the shuttle away from Tevel.

"We need to go back," Poe moaned, but Finn shook his head.

"No, we need to get you back to base."

"But the bacta . . ."

"Leia will understand, Poe. You're more important than any mission."

THE END

CAN YOU GO BACK AND MAKE BETTER DECISIONS?

"SORRY," POE SAID, drawing his blaster and stunning Varak. "We can't let you do that."

As BB-8 sent the door slamming down, Finn stunned the support officers to the sound of stormtroopers trying to override the lock.

"How are we gonna deal with them?" Finn asked, glancing back at the door.

Poe's eyes narrowed as he stared through the viewport. "One problem at a time."

The TIE fighter pilots were scrambling to the other side of the bacta plant.

WHAT DO THEY DO?

FIRE ON THE TIES—HEAD TO PAGE 73.

TRY TO GET BACK TO THE SHUTTLE—TURN TO PAGE 68.

POE RAISED HIS CHIN to match the officer's disdainful expression. "We are here to inspect the plant, Major . . ."

"Varak," the officer provided, hands clasped behind his narrow back. "Kander Varak. An inspection, you say. Under whose authority?"

"Kylo Ren's, of course," Finn chimed in, drawing a glare from Poe. His mouth went dry. Had name-dropping their old enemy been too much?

A muscle tensed in Varak's jaw. "The Supreme Leader? I must check with high command at once."

WHAT DOES POE SAY?

"THE SUPREME LEADER WILL BE DISPLEASED." TURN TO PAGE 61.
"AN EXCELLENT IDEA. WE'LL COME WITH YOU." GO TO PAGE 97.

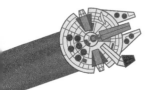

"WHAT ARE you talking about?" Poe said, trying to look as official as possible. "Your list must be wrong."

But the droid was staring at his boots. "Those aren't regulation."

"No," Poe agreed, drawing his blaster. "And neither is this."

The med droid let out a mechanical squeal as Poe fried its processor. Either the noise of the blaster or the cry of the robot brought stormtroopers running.

Finn and Poe didn't stand a chance. The shuttle was filled with stun beams, and both rebels had hit the deck within seconds.

THE END

CAN YOU GO BACK AND MAKE BETTER DECISIONS?

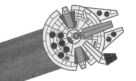

POE SNORTED. "You can, of course, but I must warn you that the Supreme Leader will be displeased. He doesn't like his orders being questioned."

"Yeah," Finn agreed, not registering the look of annoyance that flashed across Poe's face. "You should see the last guy who checked in with high command."

"What happened?" Varak asked, doubt creeping into his nasal voice.

"I don't think we need to get into that," Poe said, but Finn didn't take the hint.

"We were examining a field hospital on the Perlemian Reach," Finn said, starting to enjoy the subterfuge. "The surgeon general questioned our orders, so Supreme Leader Ren demoted her on the spot."

"Now she's mopping up bathrooms on the *Harbinger*," Poe interrupted, taking control of the conversation again. "Do you know how many bathrooms are on a Star Destroyer, Major?"

"No." Varak had visibly paled.

"One thousand eight hundred twenty-two," Finn told him, forcing Poe to stifle a smile.

"But by all means," he continued, "contact high

command. Perhaps you should ask to talk to the Supreme Leader personally? I'm sure General Hux won't mind putting you through."

Varak flashed a nervous smile. "I-I'm sure that won't be necessary. Where would you like to start?"

Finn grinned as Poe walked briskly toward the nearest tank, BB-8 rolling at his heels. "You can begin by giving us a tour of the facility. The Supreme Leader wishes for us to construct a holomap for him to review at his leisure."

Poe was certainly throwing himself into the part.

"Of c-course," Varak stammered. "Perhaps my seeker droid could assist."

Poe shook his head. "That won't be necessary. My BB unit is more than capable of creating a simple graphic."

The major regarded BB-8 with an expression that bordered on suspicion. "I hope you don't mind me saying, Lieutenant, but your astromech is certainly . . . unique."

Poe turned to peer at BB-8, who booped as if insulted.

"And what's wrong with it?"

Varak swallowed. "The colors, for one thing. I—"

"Have you ever dealt with the medical corps,

Major?" Poe cut in. "Do you know the regulation color scheme for a droid of this class?"

"No," Varak admitted, looking as though he wished he had kept his mouth shut. "No, I don't."

"And yet you were put in charge of a bacta plant." Poe tutted, marching on regardless. Finn fell in behind, although he couldn't shake the feeling that Varak's seeker was studying him. He glanced at the droid, and its glowing receptor snapped back to face Varak as the major began the tour. He showed them all ten storage tanks, pointing out the metal lattice that supported the glass, before explaining the roles of each and every factory building in exhaustive detail. Poe managed to feign interest as the major pointed out refineries and tech bays.

As Varak droned on about the production process, Finn noticed a huddle of Tevellans beside a storage hut. All three had long twitching ears and striped fur. The female of the group boasted a graceful tail that was lined with metal rings, while her male compatriots had long sweeping whiskers. The larger of the two wore an eye patch. But it was the older one who made Finn look again as he recognized the striking white stripe across his nose from Threepio's briefing. It was Karkan, the Tevellan who had first made contact with Leia.

Poe continued the pretense, asking questions about bacta quotas and delivery times. Had he noticed Karkan, as well? Finn was wondering if he should find a way to interrupt when Poe coughed, clearing his throat as if he was in distress.

"Are you okay, Lieutenant?" Varak asked.

"It must be the seeds from all that grass," Poe croaked, waving at the crops beyond the plant boundaries. "They are interfering with my allergies." He turned to Finn. "I need my medicine."

Finn screwed up his face, not taking the hint. "Your medicine?"

"Back on the shuttle," Poe prompted, nodding back the way they'd come, not just at the shuttle but at Karkan. So he *had* recognized the Tevellan.

"Of course, sir," Finn said, taking the opportunity to peel off from the tour. "I'll fetch it at once."

"See that you do," Poe called after him before turning back and resuming his conversation with Varak.

Finn hurried toward the hut, but the Tevellans had vanished, Karkan included. He stopped, looking around, and spotted a flash of orange fur darting behind tank seven. Glancing back to make sure Varak wasn't looking, Finn crept around the container to see Karkan and the others rising to the top of the tank on a hover platform. Perhaps that's where they wanted to meet him. Although, if that was the case, why would they have used the only platform? The only other way to get to the top was to climb the frame itself.

DOES FINN CLIMB UP AFTER THEM?

YES—TURN TO PAGE 71.

NO—GO TO PAGE 86.

"IT WAS NICE WHILE IT LASTED," Poe said, raising his hands in surrender as they were surrounded by stormtroopers. He nodded at Kylo Ren's intimidating holoform. "I guess we'll be seeing you soon. Can't wait."

Ren chuckled. "Let's see if you're so eager after you've spent time with our latest interrogator units." The Supreme Leader's malevolent gaze dropped to BB-8. "Speaking of droids, if Dameron and Eff-Enn-Two-One-Eight-Seven won't reveal the location of the Resistance base, then I'm sure the BB unit will oblige. Have its memory core sent to me. You can scrap the rest."

THE END

CAN YOU GO BACK AND MAKE BETTER DECISIONS?

"LET ME GUESS," Finn said as the walker lumbered forward. "You've always wanted to pilot one of these things."

"It's trickier than it looks," Poe admitted as he steered the behemoth toward the med shuttle.

"You're not kidding," Finn said, holding on as the walker tripped over its own feet, crashing down to land on top of the med shuttle.

When the smoke cleared, the stormtroopers had broken into the control deck. Finn raised his hands in surrender, kicking Poe until he did the same. This time there was no way out.

THE END

CAN YOU GO BACK AND MAKE BETTER DECISIONS?

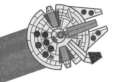

"IT WAS NICE while it lasted," Poe said, drawing his blaster and stunning Varak. As Kylo Ren ranted, Finn took down the support officers and BB-8 locked the door to seal them in.

"You won't get away with this," Ren snapped as Poe slipped behind the controls.

"Yeah, because we *always* listen to what you say," he replied, killing the connection to Ren's command ship.

Outside, stormtroopers were trying to override BB-8's lock.

"How are we gonna deal with them?" Finn asked.

"One problem at a time," Poe said, looking ahead through the viewport.

The TIE fighter pilots were scrambling to the other side of the bacta plant.

WHAT DO THEY DO?

FIRE ON THE TIES—HEAD TO PAGE 73.
TRY TO GET BACK TO THE SHUTTLE—TURN TO PAGE 68.

"JUST THE ONE?" Poe said, punching Varak in the jaw.

He yelled for Finn to run, and they raced in the direction of the med shuttle only to find a platoon of stormtroopers waiting for them.

They were surrounded in seconds, forced to raise their hands in surrender.

Varak stalked over to them, rubbing his inflamed jaw. "You're going to regret that."

"Nah," Poe said as he was led away. "I'd do it again if I had the chance. . . ."

THE END

CAN YOU GO BACK AND MAKE BETTER DECISIONS?

HE CRANED HIS NECK, looking up at the tank. How difficult could the climb be? And besides, it wasn't like he was scared of heights or anything.

By the time he was halfway up, Finn had decided that fear of heights was actually quite sensible. The steel frame was surprisingly rickety, and the duracrete ground below him looked all too solid.

But he knew that Poe wouldn't think twice about scaling the tank, and Rey . . . well, Rey would have probably done something awesome using the Force. He wasn't about to let down the Resistance, even if that meant his arms were aching and he was struggling to breathe by the time he reached the top.

Karkan and the other Tevellans were on the other side of the roof, clustered around some kind of hatch.

WHAT SHOULD FINN DO?

CALL OUT TO THEM—TURN TO PAGE 74.

CREEP OVER TO THEM—GO TO PAGE 76.

BRACING HIMSELF, Finn clambered onto the frame, his arms already aching from his earlier climb.

It was a big mistake. When he was only halfway down, the steel lattice started to buckle, coming away from the tank. He tried to swing onto another section, but his tired muscles were in a worse state than the frame. Finn slipped, his fingers losing their grip, and fell onto the duracrete ground. Now Finn was the one who needed bacta!

THE END

CAN YOU GO BACK AND MAKE BETTER DECISIONS?

"CAN YOU FIRE ONE of these things?" Poe asked.

Finn dropped into the gunner seat, trying to remember what little he'd learned about walkers during his training on the *Finalizer*. "I'll try."

He targeted the nearest TIE fighter and pressed the control, and . . . nothing happened.

"There must be a failsafe," Finn said. "They can't fire on their own."

The control deck shook as TIE fighter fire lashed the AT-AT.

"You sure about that?"

BB-8 squealed as the door slid up and stormtroopers barged in, blasters raised. "The controls are isolated," the troop commander told them. "Drop your weapons and surrender."

Finn and Poe unclipped their blasters and threw them to the floor. Their mission was at an end.

THE END

CAN YOU GO BACK AND MAKE BETTER DECISIONS?

"HEY!" FINN CALLED, still breathless from the climb. The aliens didn't look up, so he tried again as he jogged closer. "What are you doing?"

Karkan looked up, his violet eyes going wide. The alien jabbered something, and all three Tevellans dashed to the roof's edge.

"No, wait!" Finn cried out as, in perfect unison, the Tevellans threw themselves from the top of the tank. He ran forward to see them gliding to the ground like bat-squirrels, thin membranes stretched between their arms and torsos.

"Handy," he muttered, making the mistake of looking down. A wave of vertigo swept over him, and he staggered away from the edge. Why had they run? It made no sense. Then he remembered the long white coat he was wearing. The Tevellans had assumed he was First Order. No wonder they didn't trust him. He'd climbed all that way for nothing.

He straightened up, spotting something beside the open hatch. It was a small vial containing a clear liquid. Slipping the bottle into his pocket, he glanced into the

tank. His aching legs could do with some of that bacta, especially since he had to get down again.

HOW DOES HE GET BACK DOWN TO THE GROUND?

CLIMB DOWN USING THE FRAME—TURN TO PAGE 72.
USE THE HOVER PLATFORM—GO TO PAGE 82.

NOT WANTING ANYONE to hear him call out, Finn crept over to the Tevellans and reached out to tap Karkan on his boney back. Startled, the alien grabbed Finn's arm and threw the rebel over his shoulder. Finn fell through the open hatch, landing with a splash in the bacta.

Karkan had slammed the hatch shut before Finn could swim back up to the surface. Holding his breath, he tried to push open the lid, but it was locked tight. Trying not to panic, Finn banged on the side of the tank, telling himself that someone would hear him. They just had to.

THE END

CAN YOU GO BACK AND MAKE BETTER DECISIONS?

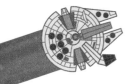

THERE WAS A BANG on the cell wall. Wincing with pain, Finn pushed himself up from the bunk.

"Hello?"

A muffled but familiar voice came through the wall. "Finn?"

"Poe!" His friend was in the next cell.

"Great prison break, pal," Poe said through the metal partition. "Any idea how we can get out of this one?"

Finn sank back onto the bed. Not yet . . . but he was sure he would think of something . . . soon.

THE END

CAN YOU GO BACK AND MAKE BETTER DECISIONS?

POE MADE A SHOW of shaking his head in disappointment.

"I'm so sorry, Major Varak," he said, glaring at Finn. "I had no idea that this . . . renegade was working against us. Have no fear that his punishment will be swift, not to mention severe." He turned to the stormtroopers. "Escort the prisoner to my shuttle. I will deliver him to Supreme Leader Ren personally."

Varak raised a hand before they could react. "That won't be necessary. We have holding cells on board the command walker."

Poe glanced toward the AT-AT standing immobile at the center of the plant. "You wish to interrogate him yourself?"

"Naturally. This is my plant. I will decide the punishment. Besides, you would be alone with the traitor. Here we have the protection of my stormtroopers."

"I have my droid," Poe argued, glancing down at BB-8, who was trying his best to look intimidating.

"We can question him together," Varak concluded. "For all we know, the traitor might be part of the

Resistance. This could be exactly what we need to crush them."

He signaled for the stormtroopers to take Finn away. Finn tensed, ready to make a break for it, but Poe caught his eye, shaking his head almost imperceptibly.

Did he have a plan?

"This way, traitor," the first stormtrooper said, shoving Finn between tanks three and four. He limped on, mentally running through the best ways to take down both troopers, injured ankle or not.

It was useless.

Suddenly, one of the troopers with Finn hit the ground! His patrol mate slumped on top of him seconds later.

Karkan emerged from the shadows, clutching the toolbox he had used to clobber the first stormtrooper. The other had been knocked senseless by the stronger of the male Tevellans, who stood behind the leader.

On the ground, the stormtroopers moaned, starting to come to.

DOES FINN ESCAPE OR HELP SUBDUE THE TROOPERS?

HELP SUBDUE THE TROOPERS—GO TO PAGE 87.
ESCAPE—TURN TO PAGE 80.

FINN WASN'T GOING TO WAIT around to be battered by a toolbox. He ran before the Tevellans could go for the troopers' blasters, darting between the storage tanks.

He heard one of them yell after him but knew he and Poe had to get off the planet, whether he had the bacta or not. Weaving in and out of the tanks, he raced for the walker, hoping he could get Poe's attention.

He never had a chance. Buzzing like a swarm of thunder-wasps, Varak's seeker droid swooped from the sky and blocked Finn's path. Finn ducked to avoid running headfirst into the seeker but couldn't dodge the stinging electro-shock prod that jabbed into his neck.

He went down hard, waking in a cell on board the command walker. Varak was standing in front of him, as smug as ever even as Finn launched at him in rage, stopped short by the restraints clamped around his wrists and ankles.

"Where's Poe?" he croaked, his throat dry from the droid's shock prod.

Varak didn't even flinch at the sound of Poe's real

name. "And we finally have the truth," he said. "We knew you'd slip up eventually."

Finn frowned. "You knew we were from the Resistance?"

The major chuckled. "Of course we did."

"Then why play along?"

Varak cocked his head as if speaking to a child. "Because we needed you to lead us to the traitors . . . the *real* traitors."

Finn's heart sank as he realized Varak meant Karkan and the others. "You were using us to root them out."

Varak faked a round of applause. "You have served the First Order well, Eff-Enn-Two-One-Eight-Seven. Very well indeed."

THE END

CAN YOU GO BACK AND MAKE BETTER DECISIONS?

THERE WAS NO WAY he was going to risk clambering back down the outside of the tank. If the frame didn't give way, his arms definitely would. He hurried to the hover platform and started his descent, the repulsors whining. Why were they so loud? Someone would hear them in a min—

"What are you doing up there?"

Too late. A stormtrooper patrol had spotted him, their blasters already sweeping up. Finn dove from the platform, aiming to drop into a roll before they could open fire. The jump didn't exactly go as planned. His ankle turned underneath him as he landed, sending him sprawling across the duracrete as the stormtroopers approached, rifles trained on him. His white coat had flapped open, revealing the blaster hidden underneath. He just hoped the vial hadn't been smashed when he fell.

There was no point fighting as he was forced to limp to the station commander. Varak had finished the tour and was leading Poe back from a *fascinating* examination of the bacta pipes.

"We found this man sneaking around tank seven," the first stormtrooper said, the second showing the blaster they had confiscated.

With a nod, Varak dispatched his seeker droid, who flew immediately to the top of the tank to transmit holos to the major's datapad.

Varak turned the screen around so everyone could see an image of the open hatch. Finn groaned inwardly, wishing he'd shut the hatch before leaping onto the platform. Just another mistake to add to an ever-growing list.

"And how do you explain this?"

"Yes, nurse," Poe said, playing along to save face. "What do you think you were doing?"

Finn couldn't admit he'd followed Karkan and the others up there, not unless he wanted to betray them to the First Order.

"I . . . er . . . I wanted to take a closer look at the bacta. For Supreme Leader Ren."

Varak's eyes narrowed. "And what about your commanding officer's medicine? Did you expect to find it up there, as well?"

Finn shook his head, fists clenched in frustration. Had he blown the mission?

The seeker droid buzzed back down to scan Finn from head to toe. It issued a series of bleeps, and Varak read the translation on his pad.

"It appears you have something in your pocket. Show me."

Sighing, Finn produced the vial, which was fortunately still in one piece. Varak snatched it from his grasp, holding it up.

"What is this?" he demanded, shaking the container.

"I don't know," Finn answered honestly.

"Liar," Varak snapped. "You were obviously trying to sabotage our bacta."

"*Your* bacta?" Finn couldn't help reacting to the man's arrogance. "It's the Tevellans' bacta. You can't just take whatever you want."

Varak grinned, displaying a row of stained teeth. "Actually, we can." Pulling a comlink from his tunic, he barked an order at his subordinates. "Have tank seven checked for contaminants. We have a traitor in our midst."

WHAT DOES POE DO?

ATTACK VARAK—GO TO PAGE 70.

PLAY ALONG—TURN TO PAGE 78.

THERE WAS NO WAY he was going to risk his neck clambering up that thing.

"What goes up must take a hover platform back down," Finn said to himself, waiting.

But he was out of time.

"Hey, what are you doing?"

Finn turned to see a patrol of stormtroopers walking toward him.

"I . . . I got lost," he lied, trying not to flinch as he spotted Karkan and the others starting their descent. Unfortunately, one of the stormtroopers followed his gaze.

"Get down from there!" the trooper barked, raising his blaster. Finn tried to stop him but was pushed back. He could only watch as Karkan and the other Tevellans tried to escape only to be stunned by the stormtroopers.

Finn groaned. Karkan and the others would never trust them now.

THE END

CAN YOU GO BACK AND MAKE BETTER DECISIONS?

THE TEVELLAN with the eye patch went for one of the stormtroopers' blasters, but Finn was quicker. He scooped up the rifle, switching modes with practiced ease, and stunned both troopers. From a distance, their armor would have protected them from the blasts, but so close they'd be sleeping off the stun beams for quite some time.

"We need to get out of here," he said, looking around. "Someone might have heard the shots." But when he turned back to Karkan, the Tevellan had leveled the other blaster at *him*. A glance at the weapon's controls told Finn that it was still set to kill.

"Where's the vial?" Karkan hissed. "We know you found it."

"I did," Finn admitted, "but Varak took it."

The Tevellan uttered a curse in his own language before glancing around at the sound of running boots.

Finn could have used the distraction to disarm him, but he needed the plant worker on his side.

"We were sent by General Organa."

Karkan's fur-covered brow creased. "Of the Resistance?"

Finn nodded. "We need to talk."

The Tevellan exchanged looks with his nervous accomplices before lowering his blaster. "Come with us."

Still gripping the rifle, Karkan led Finn through the plant, taking a route the troopers would never be able to follow. Finn hobbled as fast as he could but knew he was slowing them down.

"In here," the female said, ushering Finn into a work hut. Inside was a small control room, with screens showing various camera feeds around the facility.

"We can't stay long," Karkan said, thrusting the blaster into the female's hands before rushing to a locker in the wall. He opened the door, retrieving something Finn couldn't see.

"What are you doing?"

"Sit down," the Tevellan with the eye patch said, indicating a chair by the main computer bank.

Finn narrowed his eyes.

The female sighed. "Do you want Karkan to fix your ankle or not?"

The elderly Tevellan turned to reveal a roll of bacta-infused bandages in his hand. Finn relented, carefully placing the rifle he had snatched on the computer desk before sitting.

"I'm Tarina," the female told him as Karkan wrapped the gauze around Finn's sprain, "and this lug is Menon."

"I thought there would be more of you," the thick-set Tevellan said.

"Unfortunately, there's not many of us at all," Finn admitted. "Which is why we need your bacta."

"And you think we're in a position to hand it over?" Menon grunted.

Karkan raised a hand to calm his bad-tempered friend. "Finn came a long way to help us, even if he did lose our vial."

Menon huffed. "Help himself, you mean. The Resistance doesn't care about us."

"That's not true," Finn insisted. "And besides, why couldn't you take back the plant yourself. There aren't that many stormtroopers."

"More than enough to hold our young," Tarina said bitterly.

"What?"

Karkan placed a sympathetic hand on her shoulder. "Major Varak has our children under armed guard in one of the warehouses. If we refuse to work . . ."

His voice trailed off, but his meaning was obvious.

"The vial contains a special formula that Tarina developed," he added, smiling sadly at the female.

"What does it do?"

"It corrupts bacta," Tarina told him, her tail flicking proudly. "Rendering it useless."

89

"We were going to contaminate the bacta supplies to buy time," Menon said.

"But we need that bacta," Finn said.

"And we need our children," Karkan snapped, anger flashing across his tired face. His shoulders slumped. "I'm sorry. It's . . . it's not been easy."

"It never is when the First Order is involved," Finn said, standing to test his ankle. The bacta had already started to work, reducing both the swelling and the pain. "But we can help you."

"You?" Menon scoffed. "Two humans and a droid?"

"Let him speak," Tarina told the large Tevellan. The trouble was that Finn didn't really know what to suggest, but he knew that Poe could help him come up with a plan.

"We need to get a message to my friend. We'll work out how to free your children, I promise."

Karkan bustled past Finn, his long fingers dancing over the surveillance controls. "Then let's see where he is."

He flicked through the camera feeds, but Poe was nowhere to be seen. Finn leaned over the console, searching the screens until he spotted him.

"There he is!"

Poe and Varak were arguing in the shadow of the

command walker. Even without sound, it was clear that their voices were raised.

"He needs our help," Finn said, snatching up the blaster rifle and darting outside before anyone could stop him.

Finn was right. Poe did need help. He had been led to the command walker by Varak but knew that getting into the AT-AT was a bad idea. Reports had come in that Finn had gone missing and the stormtroopers accompanying him had been attacked by an unknown force. Varak had placed the entire plant on alert. Their cover was minutes from being blown, but Poe wanted to know what was in that vial. As they hurried toward the walker's legs, Poe faked a trip, falling into the commander and slipping his hand into the man's tunic pocket to retrieve the glass tube. Varak's hand closed around his wrist. The officer twisted, turning Poe's arm back on itself. The major was stronger than he looked.

Poe pulled himself free, rubbing his sore arm. "What do you think you're doing, Varak?"

"I could ask the same, *Captain Dameron!*"

The use of Poe's real name rattled him, but he tried not to show it.

"I don't know what you're talking about. I am a medical envoy from Central Command."

"No," Varak snapped, pointing a boney finger at Poe. "You're the fugitive who destroyed the *Fulminatrix* and a key member of Leia Organa's rebellious inner circle." He snapped his finger, and the seeker droid projected surveillance footage of Poe and Finn hiding beneath the *Rover*.

"You knew who we were all along?" Poe asked, staring at the image.

"Did you really think you could fool the First Order?" the major crowed. "We've been playing along to see what you and your turncoat friend would do."

"Yeah?" Poe said. "Then it's about time I showed you!"

WHAT DOES POE DO?

TRY TO ESCAPE—HEAD TO PAGE 114.

MAKE SURE BB-8 GETS AWAY—GO TO PAGE 93.

POE PULLED BACK HIS ARM and punched the major in his pompous jaw. Varak hit the ground, but Poe didn't try to run. Instead he dropped his shoulder and rammed into the nearest stormtrooper, yelling for BB-8 to move.

"Go on, buddy. Go find Finn!"

Beeping wildly, the astromech spun around and disappeared among the bacta tanks, leaving Poe to be subdued by the remaining troopers.

"Get that droid!" Varak screamed, and his seeker droid buzzed after the fleeing BB unit.

BB-8 swerved and weaved through the tanks, but the seeker wasn't giving up, its red lens burning with programmed hatred. Laser blasters snapped out of the probe droid's casing to send a stream of energy bolts after the rolling astromech.

BB-8 changed direction, wheeling toward a group of buildings as the seeker's blasters chewed up the ground behind him. In his panic, the little unit made a mistake, rushing between the buildings to find himself in a dead end, his path blocked by a solid wall. He turned on his

axis to see the seeker at the mouth of the passageway,
its blasters glowing hot. BB-8 responded by deploying
all his tools at once, from multiple welding arms to a fire
extinguisher.

The seeker wasn't impressed, beeping menacingly
as it swept forward. But then it exploded in a blaze of
sparks! It crashed to the ground, its circuitry sizzling
before it finally lay still. BB-8 looked up through the
smoke at Finn, whose blaster rifle was still raised from
shooting down the droid.

BB-8 squealed in delight, rolling toward the former

trooper, his various attachments snapping back into place.

"Yeah, I'm happy to see you, too," Finn said, stepping to the side before the excitable droid could trip him up. "What happened to Poe?"

BB-8 emitted a series of shrill whistles that hurt Finn's ears, though he didn't understand them.

"I'm guessing they know who we are. I knew it was too good to last." He checked the charge on the blaster rifle. "Well, it looks like we need to mount a rescue mission."

BB-8 wheeled back slightly as Karkan and the others hurried up behind Finn.

"Don't worry," Finn said quickly as BB-8 rolled back into the alley. "They're with me."

"And I'm afraid we're the bearers of bad news," the Tevellan said. "Your friend has been taken to the command walker. You can't storm it alone."

Finn frowned. "Poe would for me."

"But what about our children?" Tarina reminded him. "You said you would help us."

Finn sighed. There was no way he could do both.

WHAT DOES FINN DECIDE TO DO?

RESCUE POE—TURN TO PAGE 130.

RESCUE THE CHILDREN—GO TO PAGE 98.

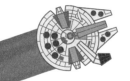

"AN EXCELLENT IDEA," said Poe. "We'll come with you."

"Of course," Varak said. "Please, follow me."

He led them to the command walker, and they rode a hover platform up to the giant machine.

Once inside, they headed straight for the command deck, and Varak ordered his petty officer to send a message to high command.

DO THEY LET HIM SEND THE MESSAGE?

YES—GO TO PAGE 39.

NO—HEAD TO PAGE 58.

IN HIS HEART OF HEARTS Finn knew what Poe would really do.

"Where are your children being held?" he asked, and Karkan smiled gratefully.

"In warehouse four. The stormtroopers have converted it into a barracks."

Finn hefted the rifle. "Then how do we get in?"

The Tevellans took Finn and BB-8 to a quadrangle of four buildings close to the docked TIE fighters. Peering around the corner of an equipment hut, Finn frowned as he saw two stormtroopers guarding the main entrance to the warehouse, each wielding a chunky stun baton.

"We've been digging a tunnel across the quad," Menon told him, beckoning Finn inside the hut to reveal a muddy hole hidden beneath loose floor tiles. "I'm afraid we haven't gotten very far."

"At least you tried," Finn said. "Most people just roll over when the First Order marches into town, but not you. You're fighters."

"Not that it's done us much good," Tarina said.

"You're being too hard on yourself," Finn said, putting down his blaster. "There must be something here we can use."

He pulled a thick drop cloth from what he hoped was a pile of equipment, only to discover a heap of old junk.

"Maybe we could try somewhere else," he said, and was about to leave when BB-8 ran over his feet to cross the cramped storeroom.

"Ow! Watch where you're rolling!"

BB-8 was trying to move a steel sheet from a bulky shape that was propped against the wall.

"What have you found?" Finn asked, shoving the scrap metal aside. It was a gonk power droid, its casing eaten by rust and one of its legs missing.

"What good is that old thing?" he asked as BB-8 babbled so fast his usual bleeps almost merged into a single note.

"You need to slow down," Finn said, raising his palms to shush the overeager astromech. "I don't understand you."

"But I do," said Tarina.

"Yeah?" Finn asked, turning to face her. "What did he say?"

The Tevellan smiled at him, the power droid's

missing leg in her hands. "He wants us to strip the gonk."

"Strip it of what?"

Tarina's grin widened. "Everything!"

GO TO PAGE 104.

POE SWUNG, and his fist connected with Varak's jaw at the exact moment the major pulled the trigger. The punch was good, but the stun bolt was better. Poe was thrown back, crashing to the sloping floor.

Varak rubbed his jaw but got back to his feet and kicked Poe to make sure the traitor was unable to move. Supreme Leader Ren wouldn't be happy that he had wrecked a walker, but the capture of Poe Dameron might be just enough to save Varak's career.

What he didn't expect was for the viewport behind him to erupt in a blaze of sparks. Varak turned to see Finn and Karkan standing on the other side of the wrecked screen, blasters aimed straight at him.

"You might want to surrender," Finn said, stepping onto the control deck.

Varak grinned. "I don't think so."

Finn shook his head. "Typical First Order thinking, right down to the—"

He never got the chance to finish his sentence. He hadn't seen the seeker droid float up behind him and his traitorous cohort. Barely operating but still loyal, the seeker jabbed its shock prods into the two rebels, draining the last of its battery to disable them before dropping to the ground itself.

Varak smirked at the stunned fighters. In the space of a few minutes, he had gone from having one prisoner to three. Yes, this would definitely please Supreme Leader Ren. Maybe he'd even get a promotion. . . .

THE END

CAN YOU GO BACK AND MAKE BETTER DECISIONS?

FINN GROANED as he realized the only choice left to him. If he remembered his training, there was an access hatch on top of the AT-AT that could be triggered if one knew where to find the hidden switch. The problem was getting up there. He could climb, but it would take too long. His only other option was to fly.

Trying not to think about what he was doing, Finn sprinted for the TIE fighters at the far end of the plant. Getting BB-8 up the boarding ladder wasn't as difficult as he'd feared it might be. The astromech used his adjustable arms to haul himself up, and once inside, the little droid maneuvered himself behind the flight controls.

WHO SHOULD FLY THE TIE FIGHTER?

FINN—TURN TO PAGE 128.

BB-8—TURN TO PAGE 108.

TROOPER TR-4018 frowned beneath his helmet as a gonk droid waddled toward them. What was wrong with that thing? It looked as if it could barely walk, let alone power anything.

As if to prove his point, the gonk came to a shambling halt. It made a couple of guttural honks and waited, as if TR-4018 was supposed to know what it was saying. Even the thing's vocabulator, limited though it was to one noise, was on the blink. TR-4018 looked over to his buddy on the other side of the warehouse door. TR-1004 was staring straight ahead, ignoring the droid. That was just typical. TR-1004 followed orders to the letter, not because he was obedient but because it meant he never had to show initiative.

The gonk honked again.

TR-4018 sighed. "What do you want?"

The droid shuffled a few steps toward the door.

TR-4018 shook his head. "Sorry. No can do. No one is allowed in or out of that place."

The droid honked and honked and honked and honked.

"Oh, let it in for Snoke's sake," TR-1004 said, finally

breaking his silence. "What difference will it make? The thing's a walking battery!"

TR-4018 couldn't believe his ears. TR-1004 was actually thinking for himself, although TR-4018 was pretty sure he just wanted the droid to shut up.

But he was right. What difference would it make?

"Go on then," TR-4018 said, hitting the door control with his elbow. The droid honked once in gratitude and shuffled in, leaving the two stormtroopers in blissful silence as the door closed behind it.

Inside the building, the gonk continued down the corridor before coming to an unsteady stop by an alcove. Shuffling around as if to make sure no one was looking, it backed into the cubbyhole before its casing snapped open, a lid popping up at the top of its blocky body.

Finn gasped for air as he stood up. He stretched, feeling his spine pop. *That is what you get for listening to BB-8*, he thought, although he had to admit the droid's crazy plan had worked. Getting inside the casing had been a tight squeeze, even with all the gonk's internal components removed, but at least BB-8 had left him with a rudimentary sound box to make the power droid's signature honk.

Clambering out of the empty casing, he ran to a side

entrance to open the door for Karkan and the others, BB-8 rolling at their heels.

"Okay," Finn said. "Where are your kids?"

The warehouse had been separated into smaller rooms, most filled with supplies and equipment. Karkan led them to the back of the building, where another stormtrooper stood guard in front of a set of double doors, this time with a blaster pistol.

HOW DO THEY GET PAST THE TROOPER?

USE THE GONK DROID AGAIN. GO TO PAGE 116.

RUSH HIM. TURN TO PAGE 135.

"WHAT MAKES YOU THINK *you're* the pilot?"
Finn asked, only to receive a litany of beeps from BB-8
in reply, no doubt at least half a dozen reasons why
Finn taking the controls would be a recipe for disaster.

"All right, all right," Finn said sulkily, dropping into
the gunner's seat and glaring as BB-8 performed a
perfect takeoff.

They streaked toward the AT-AT, and Finn aimed
for the hatch on the back of the mechanical beast. He
pressed the triggers, sending laser bolts bouncing off
the walker's armored hide.

The other fighters were already on their tail, but
BB-8 flew better than Finn ever could, a by-product of
studying Poe for years.

They shot over the top of the walker, Finn blowing
the hatch off its hinges as they came around for another
pass.

BB-8 shot an enemy fighter from the sky as Finn
leapt from the assault craft, landing with a skillful roll
on the walker's broad back.

Diving through the open hatch, Finn dropped down

into a narrow corridor on the top level of the lumbering machine. A trooper lunged at him, raising his blaster, but Finn was ready and grabbed the barrel to jerk it toward him, throwing the stormtrooper off balance.

Finn brought the rifle back up, smashing the butt into the front of the trooper's helmet, and the buckethead went down, his weapon still in Finn's hands.

"Finn, is that you?"

Finn spun around at the sound of Poe's voice. It was coming through a cell door, which Finn opened with a well-aimed shot.

"Not bad," Poe said as he bounded out of the cell.

"You can thank me when we get out of here."

"We're not going anywhere," Poe said. "Not until we bring this thing down."

"How?"

Poe ran to a weapons rack and pulled another rifle from its clasp. "How much damage could one of these do if the power pack overloaded next to, say, the walker's reactor."

Finn grinned. "Enough!"

Soon Poe's rifle was wedged next to the AT-AT's fuel pump, the power cell gradually building to a fiery detonation.

"How long have we got?" Poe asked.

"Not long enough," Finn replied. "How are we going to get out?"

HOW DO THEY ESCAPE THE WALKER BEFORE IT BLOWS UP?

RAPPEL FROM THE DEPLOYMENT PLATFORM—GO TO PAGE 112.

GO THROUGH THE TOP HATCH—TURN TO PAGE 131.

A TROOPER'S BLASTER lay discarded on the floor. Poe dove for the weapon, but he had no chance of reaching it before Varak pulled his trigger. Stun waves washed over him, and he crashed to the ground.

He had been so close . . . but Varak had come out on top. Now Poe was a prisoner of the First Order.

THE END

CAN YOU GO BACK AND MAKE BETTER DECISIONS?

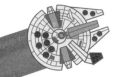

"I WAS HOPING you could tell *me*," Poe said.

Finn looked around for an escape route. "Most AT-ATs have deployment platforms. We could rappel down to the surface."

"Sounds good to me. Let's go!"

Reaching the platform meant climbing down a level and finding the equipment they needed to slide down.

"This is taking too long," Poe complained as Finn struggled into a harness. "The reactor will blow any minute."

Before Finn could stop him, Poe had opened the armored door and the wind was whipping in.

"We'll have to jump!" he shouted as a First Order petty officer appeared from the command deck.

Finn twisted, stunning her with a single shot "Are you crazy? We'll break our necks."

"Not if we do it properly!"

Finn clipped a cable to Poe's harness before doing the same with his own.

"Ready?" he asked the pilot.

Poe nodded. "Ready."

They leaned out the door, letting the cables take

their weight before jumping. They dropped, their descent swift but controlled. A shout rang out from below. Finn spun around to see a stormtrooper taking aim from the ground. He never made the second shot. Above them, the reactor blew, severing their lines and taking out the back of the walker. Poe and Finn tumbled to the ground, landing hard before the wreckage of the AT-AT came crashing down on top of them.

Some escape!

THE END

CAN YOU GO BACK AND MAKE BETTER DECISIONS?

BEFORE THE MAJOR COULD REACT, Poe swept out a foot, taking Varak's legs out from under him.

He was running before Varak even hit the ground.

"Come on, buddy!" he shouted at BB-8 as he raced in the direction of the med shuttle, but the only reply was a strangled electronic scream.

Varak's seeker droid had jammed a shock probe into the astromech and was pumping countless volts into his little body.

"Poe, move!"

Finn appeared suddenly, pushing Poe out of the way as Varak's stormtroopers fired. Blaster bolts sizzled over their heads as they sprinted for the med shuttle, Finn all but pushing Poe up the ramp.

"Get us out of here!" Finn yelled as laser fire bounced off the tiny ship's hull.

"But Beebee—"

"Just do it!"

Poe fired the engines as if on autopilot. The med shuttle launched into the air, making the jump to hyperspace as soon as they had cleared the planet's atmosphere.

"We made it!" Finn cheered, but Poe was in no mood to celebrate. They had left BB-8 in the clutches of the seeker droid. It wasn't just that the astromech held most of the Resistance's secrets in his memory; he was Poe's friend.

Would he ever be able to forgive himself?

THE END

CAN YOU GO BACK AND MAKE BETTER DECISIONS?

A FEW MINUTES LATER, Finn was back in the gonk droid, faking an argument with BB-8, who, like Poe before him, was throwing himself into the role, beeping at the top of his vocabulator.

His back on fire and his eyes streaming from the smell of burnt wiring and oil, Finn dutifully pressed the button that generated the gonk's grunts and counted the seconds until he could get back out of the box.

Fortunately, it wasn't long before the stormtrooper came to investigate the noise.

"What's going on?" he asked the squabbling droids. Finn and BB-8 booped in tandem just long enough for Menon to sneak up behind the trooper and bash the buckethead against the wall. The trooper slid to the floor, and Finn tried to flick the switch that would release the gonk's lid. It didn't work. He panicked, slamming his palms against the top, but he only succeeded in falling onto his side. He floundered inside the cube, desperate to get out, finding it difficult to breathe.

"Get me out of here! Get me out!"

BB-8 zapped the offending hinge with a shock

prod. The lid sprang open and Finn spilled out on the warehouse floor.

"I thought you said we weren't supposed to make any noise," Menon complained. "That's why we couldn't use blasters."

"You try being cooped up in there," Finn gasped, accepting Karkan's hand to get up. "Next time, you're in the droid!"

He looked around for Tarina, but she was already racing to the unguarded door. All Finn's grumpiness evaporated as she hit the control and was suddenly swamped by a wave of young Tevellans, all of whom were overjoyed to see her. Karkan and Menon joined the crush, laughing and hugging the children.

Yeah, Finn thought. *This was the right thing to do.*

Behind him, BB-8 beeped. Finn turned to find the droid opening the door to a room that had been converted to a small armory. His jaw dropped at the sight of racks of stun batons and boxes of detonators. There was enough there to equip a small army—or at least a handful of Tevellans.

They'd rescued the kids. Now it was time to take back the bacta plant.

WHAT EQUIPMENT SHOULD FINN TAKE?

STUN BATONS—HEAD TO PAGE 139.

DETONATORS—GO TO PAGE 121.

THERE WAS ONLY ONE THING to do. Finn had survived one perilous climb in the past twenty-four hours; he might as well attempt another one.

Checking there were no stormtroopers on patrol, he ran up to the towering machine. From what he could see, the AT-AT was a standard model, which meant that it had a hatch up top as well as the usual side deployment platforms. There was no way he could break in through a platform, but there was a chance, albeit slim, that he might be able to open the hatch.

After telling BB-8 to find somewhere to hide, Finn started his ascent, climbing up onto the nearest footpad. He had made it to the first knee joint, his fingers shaking from having to cling onto ridges in the metal, when a shout rang out from below.

"There he is. The spy. Get him."

He looked down to see Karkan pointing up at him. The look on the Tevellan's face told Finn why. This was revenge for not helping save the children.

Finn tried to swing around to the other side of the leg as a stormtrooper came running, but a lone figure hanging from an AT-AT's knee joint was an easy target.

Down below, BB-8 ran full speed at the trooper's shins, but the trooper's aim remained true. The stun blast struck Finn between the shoulder blades and he tumbled down, unconscious before he even hit the ground.

Finn woke in a holding cell on board the command walker. He had gotten inside after all, just not the way he'd intended. He groaned as he tried to sit up. Miraculously, he didn't seem to have broken anything, but he didn't want to imagine the bruise that was sure to be blossoming on his back already.

GO TO PAGE 77.

"WHAT HAVE YOU FOUND?"

Karkan appeared at the doorway as Finn rifled through the detonators, checking the magna-locks on the backs of the mines.

He turned, grinning at the Tevellan. "I've just worked out how to give Major Varak a taste of his own medicine. . . ."

Poe Dameron's knees hurt, although he'd never admit it to Varak. The major had made him kneel on the cold metal floor of the AT-AT's command module for at least an hour, stormtrooper blasters trained on him, but the starfighter pilot had refused to give up any information. Varak already knew that Poe and Finn were part of the Resistance, but that was all he was going to get. The frustration on Varak's increasingly angry face was worth the discomfort.

The major was about to launch into another round of interrogation when one of his officers gave an urgent report.

"Sir. The astromech. We've found it."

Poe's jaw clenched. If they hurt BB-8 . . .

"Where?" Varak snapped.

"Right in front of us, sir!" Varak rushed to the viewport. Poe knew he should stay on his knees, but he couldn't just skulk around on the floor if BB-8 was in danger. He jumped to his feet, the stormtroopers barking at him to stay where he was, but Varak waved them off.

"No. Let him see this."

Poe limped forward to see BB-8 rolling toward them like a ball down a hyper-bowl lane. What was he thinking? The astromech had always been plucky, but if Poe didn't know better, he would think the droid was going to ram the walker's armored foot.

"Fire!" Varak bellowed. "Reduce it to scrap!"

"No!" Poe shouted, trying to rush the pilot. This time, the stormtroopers did more than shout. They grabbed Poe and forced him to watch as laser bolts streamed down from the AT-AT's head-mounted cannons to blast into the duracrete around the droid. BB-8 swerved, zigzagging across the courtyard as the walker continued firing.

Poe smiled. The droid had been on enough X-wing runs to know that an erratically moving target was almost impossible to hit, especially one as small as a BB unit. Poe had played the same trick on countless Star Destroyers, weaving *Black One* in and out of blaster fire as First Order commanders fired indiscriminately, convinced of their superiority.

Varak was falling into the same trap, and for good reason. One tiny astromech against an AT-AT walker? A droid wouldn't usually stand a chance—unless that droid was BB-8!

"Ha! It's running!" Varak crowed triumphantly as BB-8 swerved into a wide arc to roll back the way he had come.

"It's heading toward the TIEs, sir," the petty officer reported. Sure enough, BB-8 was rolling toward the docked TIE fighters. Poe's eyes narrowed. There was someone crouched on the central cockpit.

Varak had seen it, too. "Magnify," he snapped, and a holographic image was overlaid across the main viewport, the walker's cameras zooming in to show a familiar figure trying to open the TIE's hatch with a crowbar.

"Finn!" Poe gasped.

"He's trying to obtain access to the TIE fighter," the subordinate reported.

"I can see that!" Varak thundered. "Take us closer."

"Sir?"

The major glared at his subordinate. "This is a walker, Petty Officer. Make it *walk!*"

GO TO PAGE 124.

THE GROUND BENEATH the TIE fighter shuddered as the command walker started tramping toward it.

Finn grabbed hold of the starfighter's armor plating to stop himself from falling as BB-8 whistled up to him.

"Yeah, you did great!" he shouted, standing defiantly as the walker approached, the crowbar replaced with his stolen blaster.

Staring down the rifle's sights, he waited as the mechanical monster stomped ever closer, Varak's amplified voice booming from the AT-AT.

"Surrender now and you will not be harmed."

Finn doubted that.

"Resist and we will open fire."

That was more like it, but Finn grinned all the same. He was part of the Resistance. Resisting was kind of their thing.

Holding his nerve, he waited for the walker to get nearer. Still his aim didn't waver. He needed the AT-AT to keep moving . . . just a few more steps. . . .

"Now!" he shouted as the walker passed tank seven.

Hidden behind the TIE fighters, Tarina pressed hard on the trigger BB-8 had fashioned from an old comlink.

Explosions blossomed around the base of the tank as the detonators Karkan and Menon had magna-locked in place exploded one after another.

The tank ruptured, releasing thousands of liters of sticky bacta. The thick liquid gushed over the AT-AT, sloshing around its hydraulic legs.

Finn lowered the rifle, smiling grimly as the giant machine lost its footing like a bantha on ice before crashing to the ground.

"Let's go!" Finn yelled to the Tevellans as he slid down the TIE's access ladder.

Fur-covered aliens ran from every direction, not just Karkan, Tarina, and Menon but every Tevellan who had worked in fear of what the First Order would do to their children.

It was the First Order's turn to surrender.

The walker's command module was a mess.

The controls were smashed, and most of the crew had been knocked out as the titanic vehicle went down.

Poe scrambled to his feet to find himself staring down the barrel of Varak's blaster. The major didn't look much better, his uniform torn and his previously

immaculate hair ruffled, but he still had his weapon . . .
unlike Poe.

Fortunately, Poe didn't need his blaster, not this
time.

WHAT DOES POE DO?

PUNCH VARAK—TURN TO PAGE 101.

PUSH VARAK OUT OF THE AT-AT—GO TO PAGE 136.

SNATCH UP A TROOPER'S BLASTER—HEAD TO PAGE 111.

"OUT," FINN COMMANDED, wondering for a moment if he'd have to physically manhandle the droid into the gunner's seat. Shaking his head, the astromech shifted position. Finn closed the hatch and dropped behind the flight controls.

How difficult could it be? He'd piloted a ski speeder, after all. Granted, he'd nearly crashed the ski speeder, but that had been on purpose.

It turned out that flying a TIE fighter was a lot more difficult than it looked. Launching the thing wasn't that tricky, although the sound of the wings scraping against the ground set Finn's teeth on edge. He even got the starfighter flying in a reasonably straight line toward the walker. No, the problem came when the AT-AT started to move, swinging around to bring its cannons to bear. Finn panicked, losing control and crashing headfirst into the walker's front leg.

To be fair, the result wasn't a complete disaster. Yes, Finn was nearly knocked senseless, but he somehow managed to get out of the wreckage before the walker collapsed, its leg buckling from the crash. BB-8 shoved

Finn out of the way as the command deck slammed into the ground, plumes of dust rushing over them.

Finn coughed, barely able to see, as a figure loomed over him. It was only the familiar voice that stopped him from lashing out.

"Finn, it's me," said Poe, limping from the walker's collapse. "That was some rescue. Come on."

Helping each other, they escaped in the confusion, making their way back to the med shuttle.

"Allow me," Poe said as Finn went to take the controls. He was happy to let Poe pilot them off-world. Their mission had been a disaster, but at least they'd gotten away in one piece . . . more or less.

THE END

CAN YOU GO BACK AND MAKE BETTER DECISIONS?

"I'M SORRY," Finn said, his mind made up.

"And that's it?" Karkan's expression was a mixture of anger and disbelief. "You're just going to abandon us?"

Finn was already heading toward the walker, BB-8 trundling behind him. "Poe needs me," he called back, scooting around the base of one of the tanks. He felt terrible leaving the Tevellans but knew that Poe wouldn't rest if Finn was in danger.

There was only one problem. How was he going to get into the walker?

HOW SHOULD FINN TRY TO GET INTO THE WALKER?

CLIMB ONE OF THE LEGS—TURN TO PAGE 119.

USE A TIE FIGHTER—TURN TO PAGE 103.

"I WAS HOPING you could tell *me*," Poe said.

Finn shrugged, leading Poe back to the top hatch. "The only way is up."

Poe climbed onto the back of the AT-AT, noticing immediately that power had shifted in the bacta plant.

The Tevellans had used Finn's assault on the walker to turn on their oppressors, fighting back against the stormtroopers.

"Way to go, fellas!" Poe shouted down at them while Finn looked around for a way to climb back to solid ground.

"Okay, perhaps this *wasn't* the best idea."

"You're not kidding," Poe agreed as a solitary TIE fighter screamed toward them.

He glanced at the blaster in Finn's hands. "Well?"

"Well, what?"

"Shoot it!"

A smile spread across Finn's face.

"I don't think he'd like that."

"Who?"

Finn nodded at the droid visible through the viewport.

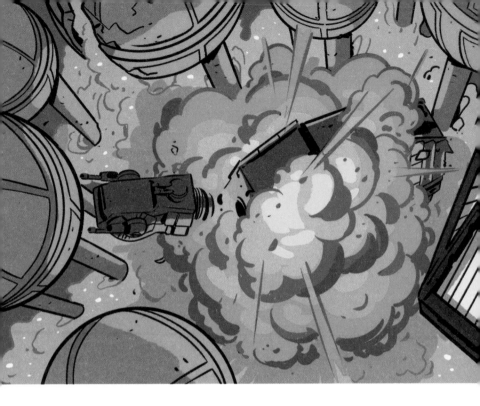

"Beebee-Ate?"

"There's only one way off this crate," Finn said, turning his back on the approaching TIE. "We jump."

"I can't believe we're going to do this," Poe said, preparing to leap.

"Me neither!" Finn shouted as BB-8's fighter screamed overhead and they bounded into the air, catching hold of the pipes and ridges in the TIE cockpit's hull.

The starfighter dipped, and BB-8 adjusted the

thrusters to counteract the extra weight of two humans hanging from the cockpit.

The command walker exploded behind them.

Poe whooped as the astromech flew them back to the med shuttle, and Finn resisted the urge to kiss the ground after they had finally dropped to safety.

Minutes later they were rocketing back into the sky, their shoulders aching and their hearts heavy, despite their escape.

"What are we going to tell Leia?" Finn asked.

"The truth. The Tevel plant is no longer under First Order control."

"Not that we'll get any of the bacta," Finn said, glaring at the stars through the viewport.

"True," Poe agreed, "but neither will the First Order. Let's hold on to that!"

THE END

CAN YOU GO BACK AND MAKE BETTER DECISIONS?

FOUR AGAINST ONE, Finn thought. *Sounds like pretty good odds to me.*

He should have known better. They rushed the stormtrooper, but the fight was over almost before it began. Tarina fell to a stun blast, and Menon was smashed against the wall. Finn would have been able to knock the trooper down if Karkan hadn't gotten in the way, making a grab for the blaster. The stormtrooper shoved the Tevellan back into Finn, and the two of them went down in a tangle of limbs.

By the time Finn managed to scramble back up, he found himself facing not just the stormtrooper they'd attacked but the guards from outside, as well.

"I knew there was something funny about that gonk droid," one of them commented before stunning Finn where he stood.

THE END

CAN YOU GO BACK AND MAKE BETTER DECISIONS?

POE DOVE FORWARD, shoving his hands against Varak's chest before he could fire. The major fell back, tumbling through the smashed viewport.

He landed on the duracrete, his blaster skittering out of reach.

He scuttled forward on all fours, only to be stopped by a calm voice as he reached the weapon.

"Don't."

He looked up to see Finn staring down a blaster rifle at him. The former stormtrooper glanced up at Karkan, who was picking up Varak's weapon.

But Varak was grinning. His seeker droid had buzzed up behind the rebels. It was battered, its circuitry hanging loose, but it still had enough power to deploy two stun prods. The traitors hadn't spotted it. They had no idea what was about to hit them.

Zap!

A bolt of light shot down from the walker's command deck, reducing what was left of the seeker droid to scrap. Varak looked up to see Poe standing in the open viewport, a trooper's rifle in his hands.

"Now," the pilot said, flashing a roguish smile, "let's talk about that bacta. . . ."

"Is that enough?" Karkan asked as Menon loaded another container of bacta onto the med shuttle.

"It'll do for now," Finn said.

"Are you sure you guys are going to be okay?" Poe asked the Tevellan.

Karkan indicated the blaster he wore on his hip. "Major Varak's troops have left us everything we need to defend the plant. Tarina might even be able to get that walker back on its legs."

"I'm certainly going to try," the female Tevellan said, her tail twitching excitedly. "What will you do with him?"

She had nodded toward Varak, who was clapped in binders within the shuttle, alongside what was left of his troop.

"We'll find a nice deserted moon for them to call home," Poe told her. "One where they'll survive but have no chance of getting back to high command."

"It's better than they deserve," Menon complained, glaring at their former captors.

"Yes," said Finn. "But we're not monsters. Not like the First Order."

"Which is exactly why we'll win," Poe said, slapping his friend on the back before heading for the shuttle's cockpit, BB-8 at his heels. "Exactly why we'll win."

CONGRATULATIONS! YOU'VE REACHED
THE END OF THE ADVENTURE!

"TAKE THESE," Finn said, handing out the stun batons. "How many workers can you round up?"

"Enough," Karkan said, testing the baton's weight.

He was as good as his word. Soon Finn was leading the charge against the First Order.

The trouble was, while Finn had been trained by Captain Phasma, Karkan's makeshift army had never fought a day in their lives.

The workers were soon overcome, unable to withstand the stormtroopers' superior fighting force. Even Finn was knocked off his feet, stunned before crashing to the ground.

Finn awoke in a holding cell on board the command walker. He groaned as he tried to sit up, wondering what fate had befallen the Tevellans. Whatever had happened to them, Finn doubted they would ever dare rebel again.

GO TO PAGE 77.

CAVAN SCOTT is one of the writers of *Star Wars*: Adventures in Wild Space and IDW Publishing's *Star Wars* Adventures comic book series. When he's not playing in a galaxy far, far away, Cavan has also written for such popular franchises as Doctor Who, Pacific Rim, The Incredibles, Ghostbusters, Adventure Time, and Penguins of Madagascar. You can find him online at www.cavanscott.com.

ELSA CHARRETIER is a French comic book artist and comic book writer. After debuting on C.O.W.L. at Image Comics, Elsa cocreated The Infinite Loop with writer Pierrick Colinet at IDW. She has worked at DC Comics (Starfire, Bombshells, Harley Quinn), launched The Unstoppable Wasp at Marvel, and recently completed the art for the adaptation of *Windhaven* by George R. R. Martin and Lisa Tuttle (Bantam Books). She is currently writing two creator-owned series and has illustrated the first issue of *Star Wars*: Forces of Destiny for IDW.